# 101 Bedtime Stories

MOONSTONE

Published in Moonstone
by Rupa Publications India Pvt. Ltd 2025
7/16, Ansari Road, Daryaganj
New Delhi 110002

*Sales centres:*
Bengaluru Chennai
Hyderabad Jaipur Kathmandu
Kolkata Mumbai Prayagraj

P-ISBN: 978-93-6156-733-9
E-ISBN: 978-93-6156-534-2

First impression 2025

10 9 8 7 6 5 4 3 2 1

Printed in India

# CONTENTS

# CONTENTS

# 1. Benny the Brave Balloon

Benny was a little red balloon tied to a cart at the carnival. He loved floating up high, but he always wondered what it would feel like to fly free.

One breezy evening, a gust of wind snapped his string, and Benny was carried off into the sky. At first, he was scared, but soon, he marvelled at the world below—children playing, rivers glimmering, and fields of flowers swaying.

He flew higher until he spotted a lonely little girl crying in a park. Gently floating down, Benny landed in her hands. Her tears turned to smiles. "Thank you for coming to me," she whispered.

From that day, Benny didn't miss the cart. He had found his purpose—bringing joy wherever he flew.

## 2. Lulu and the Shy Moon

Lulu loved stargazing. Every night, she waved at the moon and made up stories about the stars. One cloudy night, the moon was hidden, and Lulu felt sad.

"Where are you, Moon?" she called out.

A soft voice replied, "I'm hiding. Sometimes, I don't feel bright enough."

"But you light up the whole night sky!" said Lulu. "Even when you're just a crescent, you're magical."

The clouds parted, and the moon peeked out shyly. "Do you really think so?"

"I know so!" Lulu beamed. "Even when you're not shining, you're still the moon."

The moon smiled, its glow returning. Lulu knew that even the moon needed a little encouragement sometimes.

# 3. Timmy's Time-Travelling Toy Train

Timmy loved his toy train set. One night, as he played, the little train began to glow. "Hop on!" it tooted.

Timmy climbed aboard, and suddenly, the room spun around him. When it stopped, he found himself in the Wild West, surrounded by cowboys! His train zoomed through deserts and canyons, dodging cacti and being lassoed by a cowboy who tipped his hat and said, "Howdy, partner!"

"Where to next?" the train asked. Timmy clapped his hands with excitement. They zipped off to ancient Egypt, where Timmy saw pyramids and even helped an archaeologist find a golden treasure.

When he finally returned home, Timmy whispered, "Same time tomorrow?" The train gave a tiny whistle, and he fell asleep dreaming of new adventures.

# 4. The Magical Paintbrush

Maya loved painting. One rainy afternoon, she found an old, dusty paintbrush in her attic. When she touched its bristles, it sparkled.

Curious, Maya painted a little bird. To her amazement, the bird fluttered off the paper and began chirping. Next, she painted a rainbow, and the sky outside her window lit up with vibrant colours.

Every day, Maya painted something wonderful—a garden for her neighbours, stars for her room, and even a tiny castle for her toy dolls. The brush made her creations come alive.

One day, the brush whispered, "Spread joy wherever you paint," and disappeared in a sparkle. Maya promised to always use her talent to bring happiness.

# 5. Bella and the Talking Tree

Deep in the woods, Bella discovered a towering tree with a trunk covered in moss and a face carved by nature itself. When Bella leaned closer, the tree spoke, "Hello, little one. Thank you for visiting me."

Startled but curious, Bella asked, "You can talk?"

"Only to kind hearts," the tree replied.

The tree shared tales of the forest—of foxes dancing in the moonlight and birds weaving songs from the wind. Bella listened in awe. In return, she shared stories of her school, her family, and her dreams of adventure.

Each week, Bella visited the tree, their friendship growing deeper. The tree taught her that nature always has a story, if only you take the time to listen.

# 6. Captain Pip's Flying Hat

Pip, a mischievous bunny, found a strange hat in his garden one day. It was bright red with a golden feather, and when Pip put it on, the hat lifted him off the ground!

"Whoa!" Pip exclaimed as he soared over the hills, past rivers, and above trees. He spotted his friend Daisy, the duck, flapping her wings. "Look, Daisy! I can fly, too!"

Daisy joined him, and they explored the world from above. They found hidden waterfalls, treetops full of berries, and even a rainbow.

When the sun set, Pip returned home, his magical hat tucked safely under his bed. "Tomorrow," he whispered, "we'll have even more adventures."

## 7. The Kindness of Little Pebble

On the edge of a sparkling river, there lived a tiny pebble named Peb. Peb often felt small and insignificant next to the big, shiny rocks around him. "What can I do? I'm just a little pebble," he sighed.

One day, a young bird with a broken wing landed by the river. "I need to get to the other side, but I can't fly," she chirped sadly.

Peb thought hard and then had an idea. "I can help!" he exclaimed. He rolled himself into the river, settling between larger rocks to form a small stepping-stone path. One by one, other pebbles joined him.

The bird hopped across safely. "Thank you, little pebble!" she sang, her spirits lifted.

Peb realised that even the smallest can make the biggest difference when they work together.

## 8. The Sleepy Sun's Day Off

One morning, the Sun decided he needed a little break. "I work every day, shining bright. I think I'll rest today," he yawned, settling behind a fluffy cloud.

The world grew dim, and everyone began to notice. "Why is it still night?" asked Sammy, a curious little boy.

Sammy decided to write a letter to the Sun. "Dear Sun, we miss your light. The flowers can't bloom, and we can't play outside without you. Please come back soon."

Touched by Sammy's note, the Sun peeked out and smiled. "Maybe I do need a break sometimes, but I'll always return to brighten your day."

From then on, Sammy made sure to thank the Sun each morning for shining.

## 9. Millie and the Moonlight Garden

Millie loved gardening, but her tiny plants never grew. One evening, as she watered her garden under the moonlight, she heard a soft whisper.
"Try planting by the glow of the moon," it said. Millie gasped. "Who's there?"
"I'm the Moon," replied the voice. "Let's work together."
Millie followed the Moon's advice, planting her seeds at night when the world was quiet. To her amazement, tiny sprouts appeared the next morning.
Every evening, she chatted with the Moon while tending to her moonlight garden. Her plants grew tall and strong, glowing softly under the stars.
Millie's garden became the most magical in the village, and she always credited her secret gardening partner: the Moon.

## 10. The Curious Cloud

Puffy was a curious little cloud who always wanted to explore. While other clouds floated lazily in the sky, Puffy would drift low, peeking at the world below.

One day, Puffy saw a group of children playing in a field. He floated closer and asked, "What are you doing?"

"We're playing tag! Would you like to join us?" they asked.

"But I'm a cloud. I can't run," said Puffy, feeling sad.

"Then you can be the rain!" a boy suggested with a grin. Excited, Puffy let out a gentle drizzle, and the children laughed as they ran under the refreshing drops.

From then on, Puffy visited the field often, bringing laughter and rain to his friends whenever they played.

# 11. The Magical Library

In a quiet town stood an old library with books as tall as the ceiling. Ellie loved visiting, but there was one book she had never seen anyone read— the golden book on the highest shelf.

One day, the librarian smiled and said, "Would you like to see it?"

Ellie nodded eagerly. As soon as the librarian opened the book, golden light filled the room, and Ellie found herself in a magical forest. Talking animals greeted her, and a wise owl handed her a map.

"Every story you read here becomes real," the owl explained.

Ellie spent hours exploring the magical world before returning. From then on, she read every book she could, eager to discover new adventures.

# 12. Tilly and the Teeny Giant

Tilly lived in a tiny village near the mountains, where people often told stories about a scary giant. One day, while exploring the woods, Tilly stumbled upon a giant footprint - but it was no bigger than her own!

"Hello?" she called out.

A tiny voice replied, "Please don't tell anyone you saw me."

Tilly looked up to see a teeny-tiny giant peeking from behind a tree. "You're the giant?" she gasped.

"I'm small for a giant, so I hide," he admitted sadly.

Tilly smiled. "You don't have to hide. Let's be friends."

With Tilly's encouragement, the teeny giant joined the village, where everyone loved his cheerful laugh and big heart, even if he wasn't very tall.

# 13. The Lantern and the Firefly

In a small village, an old lantern hung by the door of a cobbler's shop. It had once been the brightest in town, but now its flame flickered weakly.

One night, a little firefly flew up to the lantern. "Why are you so dim?" asked the firefly.

"I've worked for many years to light the way for travellers. Now I'm too tired to shine," the lantern sighed.

The firefly thought for a moment and said, "Let me help!" It landed inside the lantern, its tiny glow adding warmth to the fading flame.

Together, they lit the cobbler's doorway every night, reminding everyone that even the smallest light can make a big difference.

# 14. Ruby's Rainbow Ride

Ruby loved rainbows. She always wondered what it would be like to slide down one. One rainy afternoon, when the sun peeked out, Ruby saw the brightest rainbow she'd ever seen.

"Come on up!" the rainbow called.

Ruby climbed to the top and slid down, her laughter echoing through the sky. She zipped through clouds, touched the treetops, and landed gently in a meadow filled with colourful flowers.

"Can I ride again?" Ruby asked excitedly.

"Anytime there's sunshine after rain," the rainbow replied with a wink.

From that day on, Ruby always hoped for a little rain and sunshine, excited for her next rainbow ride.

# 15. Max and the Invisible Bridge

Max, a curious fox, loved exploring the forest. One day, he reached a wide river with no way to cross.

"How will I get to the other side?" he wondered aloud.

An old turtle nearby chuckled. "There's an invisible bridge, but only the brave can find it."

Max took a deep breath and stepped forward, his paws landing on something solid. He couldn't see it, but he felt the bridge beneath him.

Step by step, he crossed to the other side. When he looked back, the turtle smiled and said, "Courage makes the invisible visible."

Max beamed with pride and shared the tale with all his forest friends.

# 16.  The Singing Seashell

Lila loved collecting seashells at the beach. One sunny morning, she found a shiny pink shell that seemed to hum softly when she picked it up.

"Hello!" a tiny voice sang from inside the shell.

Startled, Lila asked, "Who's there?"

"I'm a singing seashell," the voice replied. "Hold me close to your ear, and I'll sing songs of the sea."

Lila listened in awe as the shell sang about dancing dolphins, playful waves, and shimmering coral reefs. Every evening, she'd listen to its magical songs, dreaming of underwater adventures.

The singing seashell became Lila's most treasured find, reminding her of the ocean's endless wonders.

# 17. Ollie the Owl's Secret Library

Ollie, the wise old owl, had a secret: he ran a tiny library hidden inside a hollow tree. Every night, forest animals would sneak in to borrow books.

One evening, Pip the squirrel asked, "Ollie, where do you find these amazing books?"

Ollie winked. "I write them myself, using the stories I hear from all of you."

The animals gasped in delight. "You mean, we're in your books?"

"Of course! Every adventure, every mischief," Ollie said with a chuckle.

From then on, the animals loved sharing their stories with Ollie, knowing they might just end up in his next book.

# 18. The Clocktower's Wish

In a quiet town, the old clocktower stood tall, its bells marking every hour. But secretly, the clocktower had a wish—to meet the people who lived below.

One breezy afternoon, a little boy named Theo climbed up to the tower. "Hello, Clocktower! I've always wanted to see your view," he said.

The clocktower beamed. "And I've always wanted to meet someone like you!"

Theo spent the afternoon chatting with the clocktower, describing the bustling market, the singing birds, and the starry nights. In return, the clocktower promised to keep ticking faithfully, knowing it was now part of Theo's world.

# 19. The Little Lighthouse That Could

On a rocky shore stood a little lighthouse named Luma. While the big lighthouses shone brightly over the sea, Luma's light was small and flickered in the wind.

One stormy night, the waves crashed fiercely, and the fog grew thick. A tiny fishing boat struggled to find its way to safety. Luma knew the big lighthouses were too far away to help.

"I have to try," Luma said, focusing all her energy. Her light grew steady and bright, piercing through the fog. The fishermen saw her beam and safely navigated to shore.

From that day on, Luma was no longer the little lighthouse. She was the bravest one on the coast.

# 20. The Whispering Wind

Tara loved running through the fields near her house, feeling the wind rush past her. One afternoon, as the wind swirled around her, it began to whisper.

"Hello, Tara!" it said softly.

Startled, Tara stopped. "You can talk?"

"I've always been here, but you never stopped to listen," the wind replied. "Let me show you my secrets."

The wind carried her voice to a distant hill, made leaves dance in spirals, and even spun the clouds into funny shapes. Tara laughed, realizing how magical the wind truly was.

From then on, every time the wind blew, Tara whispered back, knowing her friend was listening.

## 21. Leo and the Lost Balloon

Leo was at the park with his bright blue balloon, holding it tightly so it wouldn't float away. But a gust of wind came and—whoosh!—the balloon slipped from his fingers.

"Oh no!" Leo cried as the balloon floated higher and higher. He ran after it, but soon it was out of sight.

Later that evening, a tap at his window woke him up. He looked out to see the same blue balloon! It had been caught by a tree nearby and floated back down with the help of a friendly breeze.

Leo hugged the balloon tightly, promising never to let go again.

## 22. The Kind Dragon

In a hidden valley, there lived a dragon named Ember who was unlike any other. While other dragons breathed fire and roared loudly, Ember spent her days helping animals and planting flowers.

One day, a frightened rabbit came running to Ember. "Please help! A big storm is coming, and my family's burrow is flooding!"

Ember didn't hesitate. She flew to the burrow and used her large wings to shield the rabbit's home from the rain. The rabbit family was saved, and soon, animals from all over the valley came to thank Ember.

From then on, Ember was known as the Kind Dragon who always helped her friends in need.

## 23. The Dancing Shoes

Emma loved dancing but always wore her old, worn-out shoes. One day, while exploring her grandmother's attic, she found a pair of shiny red dancing shoes.

As soon as Emma slipped them on, the shoes twinkled, and her feet began to move on their own. She twirled, leapt, and spun with perfect grace. "These are magical!" Emma laughed.

The shoes guided her to a meadow, where fairies were holding a secret dance party. "You're the star of the night!" they cheered.

When the night ended, Emma thanked the shoes. "You've shown me the magic of dancing," she said, promising to dance with joy every day.

## 24. The Shy Starfish

Sammy the starfish lived in a tide pool by the beach. Unlike the playful crabs and chatty clams, Sammy was shy and always kept to himself.

One day, a little girl named Mia found Sammy while collecting shells. "You're so beautiful, Sammy," she said, gently placing him back in the water.

Sammy blushed. No one had ever called him beautiful before. The crabs and clams heard Mia's kind words and began telling Sammy how special he was.

Encouraged by their kindness, Sammy started joining the other sea creatures. Soon, he was the happiest starfish in the tide pool, shining bright in his underwater home.

# 25. The Brave Little Raindrop

Ravi was a tiny raindrop, nervous about his first fall to Earth. "What if I splash in the wrong place?" he worried aloud.

The older raindrops chuckled. "Wherever you land, you'll bring life and joy."

Ravi took a deep breath and leapt from the cloud. He tumbled through the sky, landing gently on a thirsty flower. The flower perked up, its petals glowing with colour.

"I did it!" Ravi cheered, proud of his journey. From that day, Ravi looked forward to every rainstorm, knowing he was part of something beautiful.

# 26. The Magic Feather

In a quiet village, a boy named Arjun found a shiny blue feather by the river. When he picked it up, the feather whispered, "Make a wish."

Surprised, Arjun whispered, "I wish to fly."

The feather sparkled, and suddenly, Arjun rose into the air! He soared over fields and forests, marvelling at the world below.

When he returned, the feather said, "You have one more wish. What will it be?"

Arjun thought for a moment and said, "I wish everyone could experience this joy."

The feather broke into countless pieces, each landing in someone's hand. That night, the whole village dreamed of flying.

# 27. The Garden of Glowworms

In a dark forest, a little girl named Nina stumbled upon a hidden garden. The flowers seemed ordinary at first, but as night fell, they began to glow.

"Welcome to the Garden of Glowworms," a tiny voice said. Nina looked closer and saw hundreds of glowing worms lighting up the petals.

"Why do you glow?" she asked.

"To guide lost travellers," they replied.

Nina stayed and played with the glowworms until sunrise. She promised to return whenever she needed a little light in her life.

From then on, Nina's favourite place was the glowing garden, where magic and friendship always waited.

# 28. Lucy and the Friendly Shadow

Lucy was scared of shadows. Every night, when her room grew dark, the shapes on the walls made her nervous.

One evening, she heard a small voice. "Don't be scared, Lucy. It's just me—your shadow!"

Lucy gasped. "You can talk?"

"Of course!" said the shadow. "I follow you everywhere because we're best friends."

Curious, Lucy played games with her shadow, making funny shapes with her hands and feet. Soon, her laughter filled the room.

From then on, Lucy wasn't scared anymore. She knew her shadow was always there to keep her company.

# 29. Charlie and the Clock Tower

Charlie loved listening to the big clock tower in his town. Its chimes made him feel safe and happy. But one day, the clock stopped.

"What happened?" Charlie asked the old clock keeper.

"The clock is tired. It needs a little help," the man replied.

Charlie climbed up the spiral staircase and found the clock's gears. He oiled them carefully, turning each one gently. Suddenly, the clock began to tick again, and its chimes rang through the town.

"Thank you, Charlie," the clockkeeper said. From that day, Charlie became the official helper of the clock tower, proud of keeping its magic alive.

# 30. Emma and the Whispering Woods

Emma loved walking through the woods near her house. One afternoon, she noticed the leaves rustling, even though there was no wind.

"Who's there?" Emma asked.

"We're the trees," whispered a voice. "We've seen you visit often, and we'd like to show you a secret."

The trees parted, revealing a hidden grove filled with sparkling flowers and tiny animals. Emma gasped in wonder. "It's beautiful!" she said.

"You're kind to the woods, and kindness always reveals magic," the trees replied.

From then on, Emma became the guardian of the whispering woods, ensuring its beauty was protected forever.

# 31. Jack and the Balloon Boat

Jack loved sailing paper boats in the pond near his house. One breezy afternoon, he found a strange boat made of colourful balloons floating on the water.

Curious, Jack stepped onto the balloon boat. To his surprise, it lifted off the water and soared into the sky! Jack laughed as he sailed above clouds, waving to birds and floating past rainbows.

"Where are we going?" Jack asked.

"To adventure!" the balloon boat replied.

When the boat brought him back home, Jack smiled. "I'll see you tomorrow?" The boat bobbed gently, ready for the next day's journey.

# 32. Sophie and the Golden Cat

Sophie loved animals and dreamed of having a pet. One evening, she found a small golden cat sitting on her porch. Its fur shimmered in the moonlight.

"Are you lost?" Sophie asked.

The cat purred and said, "I'm here to make your dreams come true."

Sophie blinked. "You can talk?"

The cat nodded. "I can stay with you for one week. After that, my magic will choose someone else who needs a friend."

Sophie and the golden cat spent the week playing, laughing, and exploring. When the time came to say goodbye, Sophie hugged the cat. "Thank you for being my friend."

The golden cat purred and disappeared into the night, leaving behind a little sparkle in Sophie's heart.

# 33. Ben's Invisible Kite

Ben loved flying kites, but he often wished for a kite no one could see. One day, while visiting a fair, he found a stall selling an "Invisible Kite."

"How does it work?" Ben asked.

The stall owner smiled. "Hold the string and feel the wind guide you."

Ben took the string and ran across the field. Though no one could see the kite, he could feel it pulling and soaring high above him. "It's amazing!" he laughed.

Ben spent the entire afternoon running with his invisible kite, teaching others that sometimes, the best things can't be seen, only felt.

# 34. Lily and the Night Star

Lily loved gazing at the stars before bedtime. One night, as she made a wish, one of the stars twinkled brightly and floated down into her room.

"Hello, Lily," the star said in a soft voice. "I'm Nova. I heard your wish."

Lily gasped. "You're here to grant it?"

"Not exactly," Nova replied. "I'm here to help you shine your own light."

Nova took Lily on a magical journey across the night sky, showing her how even the smallest stars lit up the darkest places. By the time Lily returned home, she knew her light could make a difference in the world.

# 35. Oliver and the Snow Fox

On a snowy winter morning, Oliver built a snowman in his backyard. While adding the finishing touches, he noticed tiny paw prints leading into the woods.

Curious, Oliver followed them and discovered a small white fox shivering under a tree.

"Are you lost?" Oliver asked gently.

The fox nodded, its eyes wide with trust. Oliver carried the fox back to his cosy cabin, warming it by the fire and feeding it scraps of bread.

By morning, the fox had regained its strength. It nuzzled Oliver's hand before scampering off into the snow. Every winter after, Oliver saw the little fox watching him from the woods, as if saying thank you.

# 36. Abigail and the Wishing Well

In the centre of Abigail's village stood an old wishing well. Villagers often tossed coins and made wishes, but Abigail never did. She believed wishes came true only if you worked for them.

One day, while playing near the well, she heard a voice. "Abigail, you're the only one who hasn't wished for anything. Why?"

Abigail looked down into the well and said, "I don't need magic. I'd rather earn my dreams."

The well chuckled. "Wise words, Abigail. Here's a little help anyway."

The next day, Abigail found her garden full of blooming flowers—the most beautiful in the village. She smiled, knowing her hard work had made them grow, but maybe the well had given a tiny sprinkle of magic, too.

# 37. Henry and the Talking Hedgehog

Henry loved exploring the woods near his home. One day, he stumbled upon a little hedgehog tangled in some brambles.

"Hold still," Henry said, gently freeing the hedgehog. To his surprise, the hedgehog spoke. "Thank you! My name's Prickles. How can I repay you?"

Henry laughed. "I've always wanted a friend to explore with."

From then on, Prickles joined Henry on all his adventures. They climbed hills, discovered secret paths, and even found a hidden pond. Henry realised that sometimes, the best friendships come in the most unexpected ways.

# 38. Ella's Flying Bicycle

Ella's old bicycle sat forgotten in the garage, its red paint chipped and tyres flat. One day, as she cleaned it, she found a shiny silver button on the handlebars she'd never noticed before.

Curious, Ella pressed the button. The bicycle's wheels lifted off the ground, and before she knew it, she was soaring through the sky!

Ella flew over rooftops, through fluffy clouds, and across sparkling rivers. When she landed, she hugged her magical bicycle. "We're going on adventures every day now!" she said, excited to discover where it would take her next.

# 39. The Kindness Tree

In the middle of Willow Street grew a magnificent tree called the Kindness Tree. Legend said that whoever helped others under its branches would receive a special gift.

One day, Mia saw an elderly man struggling with heavy bags near the tree. She rushed to help him, carrying the bags to his doorstep.

As Mia walked home, she noticed a small golden acorn in her pocket. That night, she planted the acorn, and by morning, a tiny tree had grown in her garden.

From then on, Mia continued her acts of kindness, her golden tree growing taller and stronger with every good deed.

# 40. Benji and the Secret Stream

Benji loved fishing at the river, but one day, he discovered a narrow, hidden path leading into the forest. Curiosity tugged at him, and he followed it to a sparkling stream that seemed to hum softly.

"This isn't an ordinary stream," Benji whispered.

As he leaned closer, the water began to shimmer. "Welcome, Benji," the stream whispered. "I'm a magical stream that grants wishes."

Benji wished for his sick grandmother to get better. The stream sparkled brighter. When Benji returned home, his grandmother was smiling and lively again. From then on, Benji visited the stream often, not for wishes, but to thank it for its kindness.

## 41. The Mischievous Hat

Maggie found an old hat in her grandfather's attic. It was green with a long, floppy feather. When she put it on, the hat began to wiggle.

"Let's play!" the hat said.

Startled but delighted, Maggie followed the hat as it hopped out the door. It led her to a garden full of hidden treasures—glittering stones, colourful flowers, and shiny trinkets.

"Thank you for the adventure!" Maggie laughed as the hat settled back on her head.

The mischievous hat became Maggie's favourite companion, always leading her to new surprises and exciting discoveries.

## 42. Peter and the Giggle Bubbles

Peter was feeling glum one afternoon until he found a jar labelled "Giggle Bubbles" on his doorstep.

"What's this?" Peter wondered, opening the jar. Out floated a shiny bubble that popped with a cheerful laugh. Before Peter knew it, the whole room was filled with giggling bubbles.

Peter couldn't stop laughing. He ran outside, releasing bubbles into the neighbourhood. Soon, everyone on the street was laughing, their worries floating away with the bubbles.

Peter kept the jar safe, using it whenever someone needed a little extra happiness in their day.

# 43. Lucy and the Paper Swan

Lucy loved folding paper into different shapes, but her favourite was the paper swan. One evening, she made an especially beautiful swan and placed it on her windowsill.

At midnight, Lucy awoke to a soft fluttering sound. To her amazement, the paper swan had come to life! "Thank you for making me," it said. "Would you like to see where swans fly at night?"

Lucy climbed on its back, and together they soared over moonlit lakes and sparkling rivers. When morning came, Lucy whispered, "You're the best thing I've ever created."

The swan bowed its head and promised to return every full moon for another adventure.

# 44. Tommy and the Tickle Tree

Tommy discovered the Tickle Tree during a walk in the park. Its branches swayed playfully, and every time Tommy got close, it gently tickled him with its leaves.

"Stop that!" Tommy giggled.

"I can't help it," said the tree. "Laughter makes me grow taller!"

Tommy decided to visit the Tickle Tree every day. He brought his friends, and soon the park was filled with laughter. The Tickle Tree grew taller and fuller, shading the playground with its friendly branches.

From that day on, the Tickle Tree became the happiest tree in the park.

# 45. Ellie and the Little Raincloud

Ellie loved sunny days but felt sad for the little raincloud that always seemed lonely in the sky. One day, she waved at it and said, "You're important too! You help flowers grow."

The raincloud drifted closer, touched by her words. "Do you really think so?" it asked.

Ellie nodded. "Without you, there'd be no rainbows either!"

The raincloud began to drizzle softly, forming a beautiful rainbow across the sky. Ellie smiled and said, "See? You make the world more colourful."

From then on, the raincloud visited Ellie often, knowing she appreciated its special magic.

36

# 46. Max and the Magic Map

Max loved exploring, but one rainy day he was stuck inside. While rummaging through the attic, he found an old, rolled-up map with shimmering lines.

As soon as he touched it, the map spoke, "Where shall we go today?"

Max gasped, then pointed to a tiny golden island on the map. The map glowed, and suddenly, Max was on a sandy beach surrounded by treasure chests and parrots.

He explored caves and found sparkling jewels before the map whisked him back home. "Thank you!" Max whispered, and the map glimmered, ready for their next adventure.

# 47. Bella and the Moonbeam Ladder

One clear night, Bella saw a ladder of moonbeams stretching down from the sky into her backyard. Curiosity bubbling, she climbed it and found herself on the Moon.

"Welcome!" said a glowing rabbit. "Would you like a tour?"

Bella followed the rabbit, bouncing across craters and sliding down slopes of moon dust. She even wrote her name in the stars with a magic wand the rabbit lent her.

When she climbed back down the moonbeam ladder, Bella smiled, knowing she'd had the adventure of a lifetime.

## 48. Oliver and the Whispering Windmill

Oliver lived near an old windmill that never seemed to turn. One day, while exploring, he heard a faint whisper. "Help me spin again," the windmill said.

"What can I do?" Oliver asked.

"Bring me the wind," it replied.

Oliver ran across the fields, waving his arms and calling out to the breeze. Slowly, the windmill's blades began to creak and turn. As they spun faster, the windmill whispered, "Thank you, Oliver. Now I can sing again."

Every evening, Oliver sat by the windmill, listening to its soft, humming song carried by the wind.

## 49. Emily and the Glow-in-the-Dark Garden

Emily loved her little garden, but it always looked dull at night. One evening, she found a packet of seeds labelled "Glow-in-the-Dark Flowers."

Excited, Emily planted them and waited. A week later, under the light of the full moon, tiny buds began to glow! Blues, pinks, and yellows shimmered in the darkness.

Soon, Emily's garden became the most magical spot in the neighbourhood. Fireflies danced among the glowing flowers, and neighbours came by to marvel at her moonlit masterpiece.

# 50. Charlie and the Giggle Fox

Charlie was feeling grumpy as he wandered through the forest. Suddenly, he heard the sound of giggling. He followed it and discovered a small, fluffy fox rolling in a patch of flowers.

"Why are you laughing?" Charlie asked.

"Because life is full of funny surprises!" said the fox, pouncing on a flower that made a squeaky noise.

Charlie couldn't help but laugh too. The fox led him on a joyful romp through the woods, showing him silly-shaped clouds and playing hide-and-seek.

By the time Charlie returned home, he was smiling ear to ear, with laughter bubbling in his heart.

# 51. Sophie and the Feather of Wishes

Sophie was walking by the lake when a shimmering feather floated down and landed in her hand.

"Make a wish," a gentle voice whispered.

Sophie closed her eyes and wished to fly. The feather glowed brightly, and suddenly, she felt herself lifting off the ground! She soared over the treetops, her laughter echoing in the wind.

When she landed, the feather whispered again, "Wishes come true when you believe in them."

Sophie smiled and tucked the feather into her pocket, ready to believe in more magical possibilities.

# 52. Jack and the Jellybean Tree

Jack loved sweets, but his favourite was jellybeans. One day, while planting flowers in the garden, he decided to bury a handful of jellybeans, just for fun.

To his surprise, the next morning, a colourful tree had grown in their place! Its branches were covered with jellybeans of every flavour—strawberry, mint, chocolate, and even bubblegum.

Jack shared the magical jellybeans with his friends, and the tree became the happiest spot in the neighbourhood. From then on, Jack planted sweets in his garden, always curious about what magical treat would grow next.

# 53. Clara and the Rainbow Pond

Clara loved visiting the pond near her house, but one day, she found it shimmering with colours. "What's happening?" she wondered.

The water rippled, and a small voice replied, "I'm the Rainbow Pond. I reflect the colours of your joy."

Clara smiled and played by the pond, skipping stones and watching the ripples dance with every colour of the rainbow. The more she laughed, the brighter the pond became.

From then on, Clara visited the Rainbow Pond whenever she felt happy—or needed a reminder that joy always brings colour to the world.

# 54. Sam and the Tiny Giant

Sam loved bedtime stories about giants, but he never expected to meet one—especially not a tiny one!

One evening, while walking in the woods, Sam spotted a little figure sitting on a mushroom. It was a tiny giant, no taller than a squirrel.

"I'm too small to be a real giant," the little figure sighed.

Sam smiled. "Being a giant isn't about size. It's about how big your heart is."

Together, they built a miniature castle out of twigs and leaves. The tiny giant realised he could still be mighty, even in a small way.

# 55. Mia and the Bubble Bear

Mia loved blowing bubbles, but one sunny afternoon, one of her bubbles didn't pop. Instead, it grew bigger and bigger until it turned into a giant, shimmering bear!

"Hi, Mia!" said the Bubble Bear. "Want to bounce on my belly?"

Mia giggled and climbed onto the bear, who rolled and bounced her gently through the park. They played until the sun began to set.

"Time to go home," said the bear, shrinking back into a tiny bubble and floating into the sky.

Mia waved and knew she'd never look at bubbles the same way again.

## 56. The Lighthouse Mouse

At the edge of the sea, in a tall lighthouse, lived a clever little mouse named Marvin. Marvin had a special job—he made sure the light never went out.

One stormy night, the wind blew so hard that the light flickered. Marvin raced to the top of the lighthouse, carrying a tiny candle he had saved just for emergencies.

"Don't worry, I've got this," said Marvin as he placed the candle inside the lantern. The light shone brightly again, guiding a ship safely to shore.

From that night on, Marvin became known as the bravest mouse by the sea.

## 57. Ella's Treasure Chest

While exploring her attic, Ella found an old wooden chest covered in dust. When she opened it, she discovered a collection of tiny, sparkling keys.

"Each key unlocks a secret adventure," a note inside read.

Curious, Ella picked a golden key and turned it in an invisible lock near her bed. Suddenly, she was in a forest filled with talking animals and hidden treasures.

Every night, Ella used a different key, each one leading her to magical places. The treasure chest became her favourite discovery, full of endless adventures.

## 58. Freddie and the Flying Fish

Freddie loved fishing at the lake, but he had never caught anything special. One morning, he felt a strong tug on his line. When he pulled it up, he found a glowing fish with tiny wings.

"Let me go, and I'll take you flying," the fish said.

Freddie quickly released the fish, and to his amazement, it grew big enough to carry him on its back. Together, they soared over the lake, the fish's wings sparkling in the sunlight.

When they landed, the fish smiled. "Come back anytime for another ride!"

## 59. Lily and the Candy Cloud

Lily looked up one day to see a fluffy pink cloud floating above her yard. To her surprise, it smelled like cotton candy.

"Try some!" the cloud called.

Lily reached up and plucked a piece of the cloud. It was soft, sweet, and delicious. Soon, all the neighbourhood kids came to share the candy cloud, laughing and playing under its sugary shade.

The cloud floated away at sunset, leaving everyone with sticky hands and happy memories.

# 60. The Clock That Couldn't Stop Ticking

In a quiet little town, there was a clock that ticked louder and faster than any other. "I must keep time for everyone!" it thought.

One day, a little girl named Annie visited the clock tower and said, "You don't need to work so hard. Time will pass no matter what."

The clock thought for a moment and slowed its ticking. The town seemed calmer, and people began to stop and enjoy the quiet moments.

The clock learned that sometimes, slowing down is the best way to keep time.

# 61. Toby and the Glowrock Cave

Toby loved exploring the hills near his village. One day, he stumbled upon a cave glowing faintly with blue light.

Inside, he found smooth rocks that sparkled like stars. When he picked one up, it warmed his hand and whispered, "Make a wish."

Toby wished for his sister's broken doll to be fixed. When he returned home, the doll was perfectly mended, as if by magic.

Toby kept the Glowrock's secret and returned to the cave whenever someone needed a little extra magic.

44

# 62. The Rainbow Fox

In a quiet forest, the animals whispered about a fox with a fur coat that shimmered in rainbow colours. Sammy, a curious rabbit, decided to find it.

One misty morning, he spotted the fox by a stream. "Are you real?" Sammy asked.

The fox smiled. "Of course. My coat glows because I collect kindness. Would you like to share a kind deed?"

Sammy thought for a moment and decided to help a bird build its nest. The fox's coat glowed even brighter, and Sammy felt warm inside, realizing that kindness made everyone shine.

# 63. Daisy and the Wishing Star

Daisy loved wishing on stars. One evening, a star zipped down and landed in her backyard. "Why do you always wish on me?" it asked.

Daisy blushed. "Because you're the brightest star, and I believe in your magic."

The star twinkled and said, "You have the magic, Daisy. Your wishes come true because you work hard for them."

Daisy smiled, realizing the star was right. She still made wishes, but now she also believed in her own power to make them happen.

## 64. The Little Train That Dreamed of Flying

Rusty was a little train who loved chugging through the valley, but he often dreamed of flying.

One day, a passing breeze whispered, "Hold on to the wind, Rusty!"

Rusty blew his whistle as the wind swirled around him, lifting him off the tracks. He soared above mountains and rivers, his wheels spinning in joy.

When he landed back on the tracks, Rusty smiled. "Even a train can fly, if only for a moment."

## 65. The Invisible Umbrella

Ella found a clear umbrella in her attic with the words Invisible Shield written on it. Curious, she took it outside during a rainstorm.

To her amazement, the umbrella not only kept her dry but also created a bubble of warmth and light. When a cold sparrow landed on the umbrella, it chirped in delight at the cosy glow.

Ella realised the umbrella wasn't just for her—it could protect anyone who needed a little comfort. From then on, she shared its magic with anyone caught in a storm.

# 66. The Moon's Secret Door

One night, James spotted a small door on the Moon through his telescope. To his surprise, it opened, and a staircase of stars appeared.

James climbed the staircase and found himself in a cosy room filled with glowing jars. "These are dreams," said the Moon. "I collect them to keep them safe."

James shared one of his dreams with the Moon, who smiled and said, "Your dream will shine the brightest."

When James returned to Earth, he felt inspired to make his dream come true, knowing the Moon was watching over it.

# 67. Molly and the Jellybean Path

Molly loved jellybeans, so when she saw a trail of them leading into the woods, she couldn't resist following it.

Each step brought a new colour and flavour—red for cherry, green for apple, and yellow for lemon. The trail led to a clearing where a giant candy tree stood, its branches dripping with jellybeans.

"Welcome, Molly!" said a tiny voice. A candy gnome appeared, handing her a golden jellybean. "This one will make any wish come true."

Molly wished for endless candy to share with her friends, and the tree sparkled, granting her wish.

# 68. Oscar and the Floating Chair

Oscar's old rocking chair was his favourite spot to sit and daydream. One rainy afternoon, it began to wobble and rise off the ground!

"Where are we going?" Oscar asked in amazement.

"To see your dreams," the chair replied, floating higher. It carried him over sparkling oceans, lush forests, and castles in the clouds.

When the chair gently brought him back, Oscar smiled. "Now I know where to look for adventure."

From that day, his chair became his gateway to endless imagination.

# 69. Bella and the Singing Shells

While collecting seashells at the beach, Bella noticed one that hummed softly. Curious, she put it to her ear.

"Do you like music?" the shell asked.

Bella nodded. The shell began to sing a melody that made the waves dance and the seagulls flap in rhythm.

As the sun set, the shell whispered, "Come back anytime, and I'll sing for you."

From then on, Bella's favourite seashell filled her days with music and wonder.

# 70. The Starry Balloon

One evening, Timmy received a balloon that sparkled like the night sky. When he held it, he felt a gentle tug.

"Let's go for a ride," the balloon said, lifting him into the air. Timmy floated over the rooftops, through constellations, and past the Moon.

When the balloon brought him back, it whispered, "Keep dreaming, and I'll take you anywhere."

Timmy held the string tightly, ready for more adventures under the stars.

# 71. The Magic Library Card

Lucy loved visiting the library, but one day, the librarian handed her a golden library card.

"This card is special," the librarian said. "It lets you step into any story."

Lucy chose a book about pirates and, to her amazement, found herself aboard a ship, the wind whipping through her hair. She battled storms, found treasure, and made friends with the crew.

When she returned, she couldn't wait to try another book. Her golden card turned every visit into a grand adventure.

# 72. Max and the Talking Raindrop

Max loved watching the rain but always wondered where it came from. One day, a raindrop landed on his hand and said, "Let me show you!"

The raindrop carried Max high into the sky, where he saw clouds gathering water and forming storms. He danced on a rainbow and slid down sunbeams.

When Max returned home, he smiled at the rain, knowing each drop carried a story.

# 73. The Clockmaker's Apprentice

Liam loved watching the old clockmaker in the village square, but he never imagined the man would invite him in one day.

"Would you like to learn how to make time tick?" the clockmaker asked.

Liam nodded eagerly and spent weeks learning how the gears worked. One day, he accidentally built a clock that chimed with laughter instead of bells.

"Time should bring joy," said the clockmaker, smiling. Liam's laughter clock became the town's favourite, ringing out happiness every hour.

## 74. The Tree with Silver Leaves

Emma often visited an old oak tree in her backyard. One morning, she noticed its leaves had turned silver.

"What happened?" she asked.

"I grant wishes to those who care for me," the tree replied.

Emma promised to water and care for the tree. In return, it dropped a silver leaf that shimmered with magic. Every wish Emma made came true—but only if it helped someone else.

Emma loved using the silver leaves to spread kindness and joy.

## 75. Jasper and the Firefly Lantern

Jasper found a rusty old lantern during his evening walk. When he lit it, dozens of tiny fireflies filled the air, casting a warm, magical glow.

"Let us guide you," whispered the fireflies.

They led Jasper to a hidden meadow full of blooming flowers and sparkling streams. Jasper returned home with his heart full of wonder, knowing he had discovered a secret world of light and beauty.

# 76. Rosie and the Cloud Kingdom

Rosie loved clouds and often imagined living among them. One day, while lying in the grass, she felt herself floating upward.

To her amazement, she arrived in a kingdom made entirely of clouds, where fluffy castles and puffy sheep filled the sky.

The Cloud King welcomed her, gifting her a small cloud to take home. Rosie placed it on her windowsill, where it kept her company every night.

# 77. The Magic Penny

Tommy found a shiny penny on the sidewalk and decided to keep it in his pocket. That night, the penny spoke.

"Make a wish," it said.

Tommy wished to help his best friend, who was feeling sad. The next day, he found a way to cheer him up with a surprise game of hide-and-seek.

The penny continued to help Tommy spread happiness, teaching him that the real magic was in being thoughtful.

# 78. The Whispering Stream

Lila loved playing by the stream near her house. One day, the water whispered, "Follow me."

The stream led her to a hidden waterfall with a pool that sparkled like diamonds.

"Tell your secrets," the stream encouraged.

Lila shared her dreams, and the stream replied with words of encouragement. From then on, she visited the stream whenever she needed advice or inspiration.

# 79. Milo and the Magic Marbles

Milo found a pouch of marbles on his doorstep. Each marble glowed with a different colour.

When he rolled a blue one, it turned into a tiny pond where frogs and turtles appeared. The red one grew into a warm campfire with marshmallows to toast.

Milo spent hours discovering the magic in each marble, cherishing the wonders they created.

# 80. Ella and the Stardust Path

Ella often gazed at the stars, wishing she could walk among them. One night, a trail of stardust appeared outside her window.

She followed it into the sky, where she danced among constellations and slid down moonbeams.

When she returned home, the stars twinkled brighter, as if thanking her for the visit. Ella felt closer to the night sky than ever.

# 81. The Secret of the Mirror Lake

Deep in the forest, Henry discovered a lake so still it reflected the sky like a mirror.

When he leaned closer, the reflection spoke. "Ask a question, and I'll show you the answer."

Henry asked how to help his sister smile again. The lake showed him an image of a flower meadow.

He picked a bouquet for his sister, and her smile returned. Henry realised the lake's secret—kindness always reflects back.

## 82. The Singing Bridge

Anna crossed an old wooden bridge every day, but one morning, she heard it hum a soft tune.

"Why are you singing?" she asked.

"I hum when someone kind crosses me," the bridge replied.

Anna decided to teach her friends the bridge's song. Soon, laughter and music filled the air every time someone crossed it, and the bridge's hum grew louder with joy.

"giggle pebbles"

## 83. Theo and the Giggle Pebbles

While skipping stones at the lake, Theo found a pebble that giggled when it hit the water.

"Try me again!" it said, making Theo laugh.

The pebble led Theo to a secret cave filled with more giggle pebbles. Each one had a unique laugh, and Theo shared them with his friends. The lake became the happiest place in the village.

# 84. Alice and the Feathered Crown

Alice found a crown made of colourful feathers on her doorstep. When she placed it on her head, birds of every kind surrounded her.

"You're our queen now," they chirped.

Alice led her feathered friends on adventures through the forest, helping lost animals and planting seeds. She realised being a queen meant helping others, and she wore her crown proudly.

# 85. Max and the Balloon Tree

Max found a tree in the woods that grew colourful balloons instead of fruit. Each balloon floated gently to the ground when he touched it.

Inside one balloon, he found a note that read, "Plant kindness, and it will grow."

Max shared the balloons with his friends, spreading joy throughout the village.

# 86. Clara and the Moonflower

Clara's garden always looked lovely, but one night, she found a single flower glowing under the moonlight.

When she touched it, the flower whispered, "I bloom to light up the dark."

Clara realised that even small things could make a big difference. She shared the moonflower's seeds, and soon, gardens everywhere were glowing at night.

# 87. Ben and the Invisible Kitten

Ben had always wanted a pet, but his parents had said no. One day, he heard soft purring under his bed and discovered an invisible kitten!

Though no one could see it, Ben and the kitten became the best of friends. They played together every day, and Ben learned that friendship didn't need to be seen to be real.

## 88. The Magic Snowflake

Olivia caught a snowflake on her mitten and noticed it sparkled more than the others.

"I'm a magic snowflake," it said. "Make a wish!"

Olivia wished for her family to have the best holiday ever. That night, the snowflake turned their cosy home into a winter wonderland, complete with sparkling lights and magical snow.

## 89. Toby and the Talking Teapot

Toby was helping his grandmother in the kitchen when her teapot suddenly spoke.

"Pour me carefully," it said, "and you'll see something special."

When Toby poured tea, it formed pictures of faraway lands. Together, he and his grandmother dreamed of travelling to the places the teapot showed.

# 90. Lily and the Lantern Fish

Lily went fishing at night and caught a glowing lantern fish.

"Follow me," the fish said, leading her to an underwater cave filled with sparkling treasures.

Lily promised to visit the fish often, and together, they explored the wonders of the ocean.

# 91. The Golden Thread

Mia found a spool of golden thread in her sewing kit. When she used it, her stitches turned into glowing patterns.

One day, she sewed a scarf for her friend, and the thread made it sparkle with warmth. Mia realised her gift wasn't just the thread—it was her love for helping others.

## 92. Oliver and the Cloud Car

Oliver loved watching clouds, but one day, he noticed one shaped like a car. To his surprise, it floated down and said, "Hop in!"

He climbed aboard, and the cloud car carried him over mountains and valleys, showing him the beauty of the world.

When he returned home, Oliver felt closer to the clouds than ever before.

## 93. Sophie and the Rainbow Key

Sophie found a shiny rainbow-coloured key in her garden. Curious, she tried it on her toy chest, and it opened to reveal a glowing doorway.

When Sophie stepped through, she entered a land where everything sparkled with rainbow colours—trees, rivers, even the animals! The Rainbow King thanked her for bringing the key, saying it unlocked the magic of their world.

Sophie promised to visit often, bringing her kindness and joy to keep the colours alive.

## 94. Theo and the Talking Toad

Theo loved exploring the pond near his house. One day, he met a toad sitting on a lily pad, humming softly.

"Why are you humming?" Theo asked.

"To bring the frogs home," the toad replied. "They love music."

Theo helped the toad sing, and soon, the pond filled with frogs hopping joyfully. From then on, Theo and the toad became the best duet in the pond.

## 95. Ella and the Floating Books

Ella loved reading, but one rainy day, her favourite book floated off the shelf and began to glow.

"Follow me!" it said, flipping its pages.

Ella climbed onto the book, and it carried her into a story filled with castles, dragons, and brave knights. She became the heroine of the tale, rescuing her friends and finding treasure.

When the adventure ended, Ella returned home, eager to dive into her next floating book.

# 96. The Little Acorn's Journey

An acorn named Acie dreamed of becoming a tall oak tree. "You'll need patience," the old tree told him.

One day, Acie fell to the ground and was carried away by a squirrel. He landed on a sunny meadow, where he was buried and watered by the rain.

Years later, Acie grew into a magnificent oak, his branches sheltering birds and squirrels. His dream had come true, one patient step at a time.

# 97. Max and the Invisible Bridge

Max loved adventures, but the river near his village seemed impossible to cross. One day, an old crow whispered, "There's an invisible bridge, but only the brave can find it."

Max closed his eyes and stepped forward, trusting his heart. To his amazement, his feet found the bridge, and he crossed safely to the other side.

From then on, Max knew that courage often reveals the unseen paths.

## 98. Lily and the Starlight Feather

Lily found a silver feather glowing under her pillow. When she touched it, it whispered, "Make a wish."

Lily wished to visit the stars, and the feather carried her into the sky. She danced on constellations and slid down moonbeams, laughing with joy.

The feather brought her home, reminding her that every dream starts with a wish.

## 99. Timmy and the Tiny Train

Timmy loved toy trains, but one morning, he woke to find a tiny train chugging through his room.

"Hop on!" it whistled.

Timmy climbed aboard, and the train carried him through tunnels, over bridges, and into a world of tiny towns. He met miniature people and animals, who cheered as he passed.

When Timmy returned, he found a little train track waiting for his next journey.

# 100. The Wishing Tree

In the middle of the park stood an old tree with colourful ribbons tied to its branches. "It's a wishing tree," Grandpa told Emily. "Tie a ribbon and make a wish."

Emily wished for her new puppy to find its lost toy. The next day, the puppy returned, wagging its tail with the toy in its mouth.

Emily smiled and added a thank-you ribbon to the tree, believing in its quiet magic.

# 101. Olivia and the Secret Meadow

Olivia loved walking through the forest behind her house. One day, she noticed a trail of glowing mushrooms leading to a hidden meadow.

The meadow was filled with flowers that hummed softly and animals that seemed to smile. At its centre was a fountain that sparkled like the stars.

"This is the Meadow of Wonders," said a gentle deer. "It only appears to those who believe in magic."

Olivia spent the day playing and promised to return, knowing she had discovered a place where dreams and nature came alive.